Dear Parents and Educators,

Welcome to Penguin Young Readers! As parents and educators, you know that each child develops at his or her own pace—in terms of speech, critical thinking, and, of course, reading. Penguin Young Readers recognizes this fact. As a result, each Penguin Young Readers book is assigned a traditional easy-to-read level (1–4) as well as a Guided Reading Level (A–P). Both of these systems will help you choose the right book for your child. Please refer to the back of each book for specific leveling information. Penguin Young Readers features esteemed authors and illustrators, stories about favorite characters, fascinating nonfiction, and more!

Cork & Fuzz: No Fooling

LEVEL **3**

GUIDED READING LEVEL **J**

This book is perfect for a **Transitional Reader** who:
- can read multisyllable and compound words;
- can read words with prefixes and suffixes;
- is able to identify story elements (beginning, middle, end, plot, setting, characters, problem, solution); and
- can understand different points of view.

Here are some **activities** you can do during and after reading this book:
- Adding –ing to Words: One of the rules when adding –ing to words is, when a word ends with an –e, take off the –e and add –ing. With other words, you simply add the –ing ending to the root word. The following words are –ing words in this story. On a separate piece of paper, write down the root word for each word: *coming, going, helping, following, fooling, tasting.* Next, add –ing to the following words from the story: *find, move, open, roll, save, snow.*
- Character's Feelings: In the beginning of the story, Cork feels scared and Fuzz feels brave when they start out on their adventure. Discuss how each character's feelings change throughout the story.

Remember, sharing the love of reading with a child is the best gift you can give!

—Bonnie Bader, EdM
   Penguin Young Readers program

*Penguin Young Readers are leveled by independent reviewers applying the standards developed by Irene Fountas and Gay Su Pinnell in *Matching Books to Readers: Using Leveled Books in Guided Reading,* Heinemann, 1999.

For Kelly, Stacy, Tom and Steve.
Remembering Chipper. Good dog.—DC

To Faith, whose spirit and courage
are an inspiration—LM

PENGUIN YOUNG READERS
Published by the Penguin Group
Penguin Group (USA) LLC, 375 Hudson Street, New York, New York 10014, USA

USA | Canada | UK | Ireland | Australia | New Zealand | India | South Africa | China

penguin.com
A Penguin Random House Company

Text copyright © 2012 by Dori Chaconas. Illustrations copyright © 2012 by Lisa McCue. All rights
reserved. Previously published in hardcover in 2012 by Penguin Young Readers. This paperback edition
published in 2014 by Penguin Young Readers, an imprint of Penguin Group (USA) LLC,
345 Hudson Street, New York, New York 10014. Manufactured in China.

Library of Congress Control Number: 2011046755

ISBN 978-0-14-242262-5   10 9 8 7 6 5 4 3 2 1

CORK & FUZZ

No Fooling

by Dori Chaconas
illustrated by Lisa McCue

Penguin Young Readers
An Imprint of Penguin Group (USA) LLC

Chapter 1

Cork was a short muskrat.

He liked adventures.

He liked small adventures.

Most of his adventures were

very safe.

Fuzz was a tall possum.

He liked adventures.

He liked big adventures.

Most of his adventures got

him into trouble.

Two best friends.

One thought about being careful.

The other one did not think at all.

One winter morning,

Cork came out of his house.

The whole woods were white

with the first snow.

"Yippee!" Cork yelled.

He skipped in the snow.

He hopped in the snow.

He even rolled in the snow.

He ran to Fuzz's yard.

"Fuzz!" Cork called up into the tree.

"Fuzz! Come down and play!"

Fuzz stuck his nose out of his house.

"Cork," he said.

"There is something white
all over the trees."

"It is snow," Cork said.

Fuzz climbed down the tree.

"It is cold," Fuzz said.

"It is snow," Cork said.

Fuzz pointed to the ground.

"What is that?" Fuzz asked.

"Snow!" Cork said.

"No fooling."

"I know that!" Fuzz said.

"What is that *in* the snow?"

Cork looked at the ground.

"Those are animal tracks," he said.

"Tracks?" Fuzz asked.

"Who made those tracks?"

"Not me," Cork said.

"Not you."

"We can follow them," Fuzz said.
"We can have a big adventure!"
Cork backed away from the tracks.
Then he asked Fuzz, "What
if we find something
dangerous?"

Chapter 2

"Tracks are not dangerous,"
Fuzz said.

"They are only holes in the snow."

"But what if the animal that
made the tracks is dangerous?"
Cork asked.

"What if it has sharp claws?"

"You have sharp claws," Fuzz said.

"You are not dangerous."

"What if it has sharp teeth?"
Cork asked.

"I have sharp teeth," Fuzz said.

"I am not dangerous."

Cork backed away a little more.

"It will be okay," Fuzz said.

"No fooling?" asked Cork.

"No fooling," said Fuzz.

Fuzz followed the tracks.

Cork did not want to follow,

but he did.

The tracks disappeared

into the bushes.

Fuzz disappeared

into the bushes, too.

"Uh-oh," Cork said.

"What if there is something

dangerous in the bushes?"

Then Fuzz yelled, "Help!

A thing with sharp claws

has got me!"

Cork jumped.

His heart thumped.

"Oh! Oh! Oh!" Cork said.

A fuzzy rabbit hopped out

of the bushes.

Then a fuzzy Fuzz hopped out

of the bushes.

"I fooled you!" Fuzz said.

"It was only a rabbit."

"That was not funny!" Cork said.

"I thought it was funny," Fuzz said.

"Come and see.

There are more tracks over here."

Fuzz pulled Cork into the bushes.

"We can follow the tracks

from here," Fuzz said.

"I do not want to follow the tracks,"
Cork said.

But Fuzz was already following them.

He followed them behind

a large drift of snow.

"Fuzz! Where are you?" Cork called.

"I do not like it

when I cannot see you.

I am not fooling!"

Then Fuzz yelled out.

He yelled louder than before.

"Help! A thing with sharp teeth has

got me!"

Chapter 3

Cork jumped.

His heart thumped.

"Oh! Oh! Oh! Fuzz! Fuzz!"

A fat-tailed squirrel ran out

from behind the snow drift.

A skinny-tailed Fuzz ran out

from behind the snow drift.

"I fooled you again!" Fuzz said.

"It was only a squirrel."

Cork stamped his foot in the snow.

"That is not funny!" he said.

"It was not funny the first time.

It is not funny the second time!"

"Okay," Fuzz said.

"I will not do it again."

"No fooling?" Cork said.

"No fooling," Fuzz answered.

"But I found tracks again.

These tracks are bigger

than rabbit tracks.

They are bigger

than squirrel tracks."

"It is not a good idea to follow

big tracks," Cork said.

"Are you afraid?" Fuzz asked.

Cork stamped his foot again.

"No," he said.

"I just like to be careful."

"Come on!" Fuzz said.

Fuzz followed the big tracks
into a thicket.

Cork groaned when Fuzz
disappeared again.

"Help!" Fuzz yelled.

"A wolf has got me!

A yellow wolf with sharp claws
and sharp teeth!

Help me, Cork!"

Cork sighed.

"You are not going

to fool me again," he called.

But Fuzz yelled louder.

This time Fuzz sounded

really, really scared.

"HELP ME, CORK!"

Chapter 4

"I am coming, Fuzz!" Cork yelled.

Before Cork could get to the thicket,

Fuzz tumbled out.

Then a big yellow puppy

tumbled out.

Fuzz landed on his stomach.

The puppy landed on Fuzz.

The puppy licked Fuzz's ear.

"The wolf is tasting me!" Fuzz
yelled, his eyes tightly shut.
"I will save you!" Cork cried.
Cork saw a big stick.
He yanked at it.
The snowy stick slipped out of
Cork's paws.
It sailed into the air.
The puppy jumped off Fuzz and
caught the stick.

"Can you sit up?" Cork called to Fuzz.

Fuzz did not move.

Fuzz did not open his eyes.

But the puppy heard the word "sit."

The puppy sat.

"That is strange," Cork said.

"Roll over," Cork said to Fuzz.

"Roll over and look

at the strange wolf."

Fuzz did not roll over.

Fuzz did not look.

But the puppy heard the words

"roll over."

The puppy rolled over.

"That is very, very strange,"

Cork said.

Fuzz pulled his nose out of the snow.

"I want to go home," he said.

The puppy heard the words
"go home."

He bounced up.

He ran off through the snow.

"Is the yellow wolf gone?"

Fuzz asked, opening his eyes.

Cork thought about how Fuzz had

fooled him.

Cork thought about fooling Fuzz.

He could say the wolf was

big and hungry.

He could say he scared

the wolf away.

But then he thought about

being a good friend.

"The yellow wolf is gone," Cork said,

helping his friend up.

"Come with me.

We will follow some more tracks."

"I was not afraid of that yellow wolf,"

Fuzz said.

"But I do not want to follow

any more tracks."

"We will follow our own tracks,"

Cork said.

"We will follow them home."

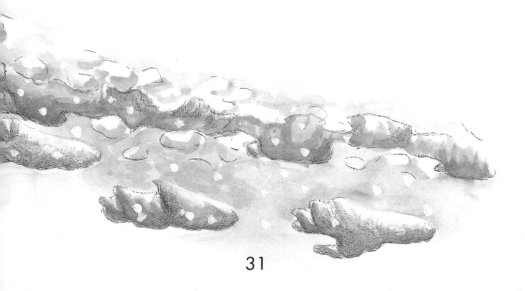

And so they did.

They skipped in the snow.

They hopped in the snow.

They even rolled in the snow.

Two best friends.

No fooling.